Tea for Me, Tea for You

Laura Rader

HarperCollins*Publishers*

Tea for Me, Tea for You

Manufactured in China. All rights reserved.
www.harperchildrens.com

Library of Congress Cataloging-in-Publication Data
Rader, Laura.   Tea for me, tea for you /
by Laura Rader— 1st ed.   p.   cm.
Summary: A tea party for one in Swinings Tea Room quickly
becomes tea for ten, as one little pig is joined by all of her friends.
ISBN 0-06-008633-5 — ISBN 0-06-008634-3 (lib. bdg.)
[1. Pigs—Fiction.   2. Tea—Fiction.   3. Parties—Fiction.   4. Counting.
5. Stories in rhyme.]   I. Title.
PZ8.3.R1175 Te   2003   [E]—dc21   2002024230   CIP   AC
Typography by Carla Weise
1 2 3 4 5 6 7 8 9 10   ❖   First Edition

In loving memory of
L. Renee Landauer

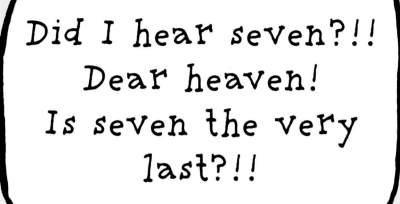

RYE FREE READING ROOM
1061 BOSTON POST ROAD
RYE, NY 10580
(914) 967-0480